Skulduggery

Tony Robinson

With illustrations by
Jamie Smith

Barrington Stoke

Published in 2014 in Great Britain by
Barrington Stoke Ltd
18 Walker Street, Edinburgh, EH3 7LP

www.barringtonstoke.co.uk

This story was first published in a different form
in *Silver Jackanory* (Penguin, 1991)

A CIP catalogue record for this book is available
from the British Library upon request

The lyrics on p75 are from *Songs of the
Newfoundland Outports*, collected by Kenneth Peacock
(National Museum of Canada, 1965)

ISBN: 978-1-78112-408-6

Printed in China by Leo

This book has dyslexia friendly features

1046672

For my lovely granddaughter Lyla.
Hopefully it won't be long before you find out
what fun books can be.

6·12·19

Contents

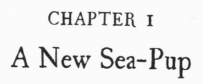

CHAPTER I
A New Sea-Pup

I stood at the gate of my new school and checked my uniform over with pride.

A jaunty red spotted handkerchief was tied round my head. My mole-skin sea boots, buckled belt and golden earring were spick and span. My blue and white striped shirt had not a single blood-stain on it.

A sign creaked above my head. It said –

SQUIRE TRELAWNEY'S
SCHOOL FOR YOUNG SEA DOGS
Head Teacher – Mistress Baker

'Twas my first day at pirate school and my heart swelled with pride as I swung my sea-chest upon my back and pushed open the great wooden gates.

But pride turned to dismay at what I saw before me.

There were no planks for walk-the-plank classes! No yard-arms where we could hang our foes!

There was only a common playground like any other playground, full of small groups of young students in white shirts, red ties and grey flannel trousers. Horror upon horrors, some of them were skipping with ropes!

And then I beheld it – the flag which makes every pirate heart swell with pride.

CHAPTER 2
The Jolly Roger

The skull and cross-bones fluttered merrily from a mast behind the crumbling school building.

I skirted round the school as fast as I could. Between a motley collection of dustbins and a small hut marked with the words "Drama Studio", there was a small harbour.

Tied up there was the sweetest 200-ton man-o'-war I had ever seen.

I raced up the gangplank and opened a hatch. Below decks, there was a stink of skulduggery.

I crept down a flight of creaky steps into the darkness. Beams stained with smoke brushed my head, and the groans of the timbers echoed down the gangways. Then ... Dee-dump! Ahead of me I heard an eerie limping sound. Dee-dump! Dee-dump! Dee-dump!

My blood froze as the sound drew closer. I flattened myself against the greasy oak wall and jumped as I felt a lump press into my back. When my terror passed, I discovered it was a door handle.

I turned it and a door swung open without a sound. I stepped into a pitch-dark cabin and waited. The limping steps reached my hiding place, paused, then moved off again. I was safe.

"Gotcha!" A hand clawed at my face.

"Snoopin' were ye?" Two more hands grabbed my arms and pulled them hard behind my back so that my sea-chest crashed to the ground.

I turned round and laid eyes on two of the most horrid young school boys I had ever seen.

One had the face of a skeleton and spectacles with lenses that were six inches thick. The other was a pale creature with skin like candle-wax and a bandage round two fingers of his left hand.

I watched in horror as he began to poke my sea-chest.

"Full of bits and baubles, I'll be bound," the other sneered.

"Nay!" I said. "Two silver pistols, a bag of gold coins and my father's treasure maps." I glanced down at the key I kept hidden on a chain round my neck.

In a trice, 8 broken finger nails and a bandage tore the key from me.

I cried out in despair. My first day, and all my worldly goods were to be lost.

At that moment the room filled with light.

CHAPTER 3
Two Pieces of Silver

"Half-blind Pew! Black Dog!" a tall, proud woman snapped. "How many times do I have to tell ye, this boat is out of bounds! Now return this boy's sea-chest and key at once!"

The rogues obeyed her with sullen faces.

"Sorry, Mistress," they whined. "We thought he were a-trespassing." And they slunk off into the shadows.

"You must be Ben," the headmistress went on – for indeed, it was she. "Take no heed of Pew," she said. "He's a kind boy really. Indeed, I have arranged for you to share a study. Come, I'll show you the lie of the land."

We left the man-o'-war and made our way across the harbour to the school.

"You have joined us at a time of great change," she told me. "In order for this school to make some real money, this harbour is to be transformed. In three weeks' time, it will no longer be a grubby backwater. No, 'twill become 'Squire Trelawney's Pirate World'. Folk will come from far and wide to witness how the world was when pirates sailed the Spanish Main. For the cost of two pieces of silver they will play at pirates for a whole day, with free lunch and a trip round the harbour included."

"Play at pirates!" I protested. "But pirating's a serious business."

"Indeed it is," the headmistress
agreed. "But times have changed.
Schools have no money and pirates must
learn new skills."

As we entered the school, I saw how
far she had lost faith in the old ways.

Her young students drank no rum and sang no sea-shanties. They had their noses stuck in books on business studies and property markets, and their teachers lectured them on banking and the law.

"If my school is to prosper, it must turn out pirates for today's world," Mistress Baker said. "That is the purpose of modern education."

CHAPTER 4
Shiver Me Timbers

Mistress Baker had me change my pirate garb for grey flannels, and then she left me outside the door of the vile Pew's study. I knocked, swallowed hard and entered. A snoozing body rocked to and fro in a hammock. I waited for a fresh attack upon my sea-chest, but none came.

"Shiver me timbers!" a friendly voice chuckled. "It's the new sea-pup!"

The body in the hammock pulled itself up and took my hand in a firm grasp. I saw a face of about 12 years old, a little like a ham with intelligent eyes.

"Short John Silver at your service," he said.

"But I'm to share with Half-blind Pew," I stuttered.

"Well, Pew's a slippery swab," Short John said. "I believe the pair of ye have already had a set-to. So I said to myself, 'Let honest John be young Ben's shipmate'."

I felt a mighty relief at my new friend's kindness and I told him how fearful I was that Pew still had his eye on my sea-chest.

Short John leaned over and pressed a panel in the wall. Without a sound it slid open to reveal a large hidey-hole.

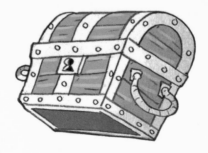

"Stow it here," he said. "It'll be our little secret. As snug as a crab in a cockle shell."

I sat spellbound while Short John told me tales of his adventures in the workhouse and at reform school.

Then a bell rang and I rushed back to the harbour, where Mistress Baker was to inform me of my duties. I was a mite peeved to discover there would be no chance to practise sword-fighting or keel-hauling.

Instead I was asked to assist in building a box-office for the new Pirate World. Of course I would rather have been swinging across a man-o'-war with a dagger between my teeth, but the tasks were pleasing enough.

I numbered the tickets myself, and
by evening I was tired and pleased with
my labours. I rushed back to my room,
eager to hear more of Short John Silver's
yarns.

But no smiling face welcomed me.
I was greeted only by an empty hidey-
hole. Short John's plan had been in vain.

I scoured the school for the coward Pew, and at last my search was rewarded by the sight of my two foes scuttling across to the man-o'-war.

In their hands were a hammer, a chisel and my father's sea-chest.

CHAPTER 5

Fifteen Men on a Dead Man's Chest

Across the wharf I crept, and once more I boarded the ship.

A shaft of light from below deck showed me the way the vile pair had gone.

With a clever knife I had purchased from a captain in the Swiss Army, I forced two planks apart a crack and put my eye to the hole. Below me was a sight I shall never forget.

It was a secret room, full to the brim of pirate garb – hats, boots, hooks and eye-patches. There were piles of wicked weapons – cutlasses, daggers and two-headed boarding axes. And Pew and Black Dog stood in the middle of this bounty, hacking at my chest.

Then a dreadful sound caused them to stop their activities. Dee-dump! Dee-dump! The limping figure came nearer, still hidden in the shadows.

"We've a-lifted his box, Captain," Black Dog whispered.

"That snivellin' sea-slug'll be crying his-self to sleep for the loss of it," Pew added. It was clear he was no judge of character.

"Our little plan's a-comin' on a treat," Black Dog gloated, and he bent his head over his chisel again.

The limping man spoke no words, but he whistled "Fifteen Men on a Dead Man's Chest".

I was all wonder. Who was this shadowy captain who could make the vilest of school boys bow down to him?

I forced my spy-hole open wider to catch sight of his face, but just at that moment Black Dog took a severe blow on the thumb with his hammer. He threw his head back, with a mighty oath, and spotted my face above him. He let out a stream of curses and hurled the hammer at my face.

To my relief, the force of the hammer was broken by a stuffed parrot hanging from the timbers and I ran for dear life across the boat. I had to find Mistress Baker and warn her that a dastardly plan was being hatched right under her poop deck.

I was about to knock on her study door when a cry caused me to pause.

"Spare me, Squire!" The headmistress was weeping and sobbing.

" 'Tis not I that does this, Mistress Baker," a gruff, heartless voice replied. " 'Tis the law. If the school cannot make money, it must be closed tomorrow."

"But I can make it pay!" Mistress Baker cried. "Once Pirate World is opened I will even have the gold to buy textbooks for the new term."

"Once Pirate World is opened," the gruff voice crowed, "I won't need a school. I'll flatten it and use the space to park the visitors' carriages."

The gruff voice must belong to Squire
Trelawney!

"Wait!" the headmistress pleaded.
"I have a new student, a foolish boy
who knows not his head from a packet
of lard. He has a sea-chest with a pair
of silver pistols and a bag of gold. I'll
confiscate them and give them to you

if only you'll spare my school. What do you say?"

I did not wait to hear the Squire's answer. There were villains all around me – even Mistress Baker was after the contents of my sea-chest. I must seek out my one true friend in the world – Short John Silver.

CHAPTER 6
Short John Silver

I sped to my study and slammed the
door behind me.

"Gotcha!" It was the vile voice of
Black Dog.

I cursed myself for the ass I had
been. In my hurry I had failed to spy my
two enemies hiding on either side of the
door.

"The treasure maps – where are
they?" Half-blind Pew hissed. "You took
them out the box, didn't ye?" He twisted
my arm and my eyes watered.

"That I did," I said. "And I stored them in a cunning place where you will never find them." I glared at him with all the bravery I could muster.

And then –

Dee-dump! Dee-dump! I heard the dread sound draw closer, like the grave.

" 'Tis the captain," said Black Dog with a wolfish grin. "He'll winkle it out of you, by thunder he will!"

The door opened and my mouth fell open in wonder. All was revealed. I had never seen Short John Silver standing up before, and there he was – one leg of human flesh, the other not there at all, so that he walked with the aid of an enormous crutch.

And, wonder of wonders, he had my treasure maps in his hand.

"How in the name of the devil did you find them?" I gasped.

"They were under your pillow, dolt," my so-called friend replied. "A drunken cuttlefish could have come up with a better hiding-place. Take 'em, boys. If you blab to Mistress Baker, Ben, it'll be Davy Jones's Locker for you."

Fear gripped my heart. I wanted my own locker, not someone else's.

"Mistress Baker would be no help," I retorted. "She, too, is after my sea-chest. For the Squire will close the school tomorrow unless she finds some means of providing him with money."

"Tomorrow!" exploded my assailants in horror. Then Silver turned and fled the room.

Chapter 7
Yo-Ho-Ho!

Dee-dump, dee-dump, dee-dump –
Silver sped down the corridor.

"Israel Hands," he bawled. "Billy
Bones! Job Anderson! Stir yourselves
from your slumbers! New orders –
we sail tonight!"

Even as he spoke, boys and girls burst from their room and followed him hotfoot to the ship. They threw off

their ties, shirts and flannel trousers as they ran. Soon twenty lads and lasses were racing up the gangplank, dressed only in their underwear.

Hotfoot I ran after them, desperate to find my chest. They dived below deck and in a trice came back in pirate garb. I was no longer surrounded by school children. Nay, twenty fearsome buccaneers were now swarming up the rigging.

"We had planned this little jaunt for three weeks from now," Short John yelled. He was now transformed into a pirate captain.

"Let modern schooling go hang," he said. "What need do we have for fancy Pirate Worlds when the high seas beckon? Baker and her money-making plans can rot in hell. With your treasure maps to guide us, we will sail the seven seas and bow and scrape to no man. Are you with us, Ben, or shall we toss you to the sharks?"

Before I had time to think, I spied
Mistress Baker running across the
harbour. "Come back, boys – remember
your education!" she called.

The ship strained at its mooring
rope and I lifted a cutlass to hack it free.
"Not you too, Ben Gunn," Mistress Baker
bellowed. "I have need of your sea-chest."

I brought the blade down with a crash. The ship swung out to sea, the sails billowed and the crew began to sing an eerie pirate song.

"Overtaken now at last

I must die, I must die

And into prison cast

And sentence being passed ..."

Short John Silver put his arm round me and his smile shone upon me once more.

"Ben Gunn," he said. "We'll be the best of mates for ever and ever."

And as I looked into his clear blue eyes, I knew that he would never let me down.

And was I correct to trust my friend? You will need to read, watch or listen to *Treasure Island* by Robert Louis Stevenson to discover the answer.

Our books are tested
for children and young people by
children and young people.

Thanks to everyone who consulted on
a manuscript for their time and effort in
helping us to make our books better
for our readers.

AHOY, ME HEARTIES!

19th September is Talk Like a Pirate Day.
But you can talk like a pirate every day!

"Aye aye, Captain!"
I understand and I will do what
you say!

"Yo-ho-ho!"
This means nothing at all
but is lots of fun to say!

"Ye scurvy dogs!"
You nasty people!

"Shiver me timbers!"
Well, I never!

"Davy Jones's Locker!"
The bottom of the sea – where drowned sailors go.

"Splice the mainbrace!"
Let's enjoy a glass of squash (or two)!

"Ye hornswaggling bilge rats!"
You cheating so-and-sos!

"Hoist the Jolly Roger!"
Raise the pirate flag and attack!

"Walk the plank, landlubber!"
Walking the plank is a very nasty pirate punishment.